StinkyKid Skye

Collecting stickers is one of Skye's favorite h[...] draw the best mermaids in her class and alw[...] and cheese sandwiches for lunch. She likes to [...] with her friend Joey so she can be a real chef someday.
Leader of Good quality: Keeping in touch with friends and family.

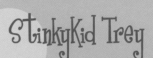

StinkyKid Trey

The golfer of the bunch, Trey is also great at building cool objects out of clay. He likes to take pictures of the places he visits with his big sister Hannah and will sometimes share his French fries with her on their travels.
Leader of Good quality: Caring for the environment.

StinkyKid Hannah

As a future wedding dress designer, Hannah loves to build houses of cards. She creates wonderful puppet shows and serves Granny Smith apples as a snack.
Leader of Good quality: Teaching right from wrong.

StinkyKid Max

A compassionate and caring person, he wants to make people smile by being a professional cartoonist. Max loves to play soccer with his best friend Johnny, and he can do ten chin-ups on his chin-up bar in under one minute. He enjoys a good kosher pickle after his hard work.
Leader of Good quality: Volunteering his services.

StinkyKid Joey

While her doggie Clyde relaxes in the sun, Joey loves to practice hula hooping while wiggling her ears in her backyard. She wants to own an adopt-a-pet shop some day and will serve doggie doughnuts to her furry clients. (Doughnuts are her favorite!)
Leader of Good quality: Compassion towards animals.

StinkyKids
and the Runaway Scissors

by Britt Menzies

Illustrated by Greg Hardin and John Trent

To the original StinkyKids, Max and Emma.
Thank you for inspiring me to create the StinkyKids characters. I love you!!

To my husband and best friend.
Thank you for supporting my journey and for your enjoyment of my art!! I love you!!

To my family, friends, and everyone who believed in my mission
to create characters who celebrate just being a kid!!
Thank you for helping me achieve success!!

. . . .

Text ©2011 Menzies, Britt

StinkyKids® characters and likenesses are trademarks of and copyrighted by StinkyKids, LLC.
All rights reserved. For information about permission to reproduce selections from this book,
write to: Permissions, Raven Tree Press, a Division of Delta Systems Co., Inc., 1400 Miller Parkway,
McHenry, IL 60050 www.raventreepress.com

Menzies, Britt.

    StinkyKids® and the Runaway Scissors / written by Britt Menzies; illustrated by Greg Hardin
and John Trent —1 ed. — McHenry, IL ; Raven Tree Press, 2011.

    p. ; cm.

    SUMMARY: The 'little stinKers' try their best to help Britt with her secret.
        Along they way, they learn that sometimes, some secrets need
        a parent's help to solve.

ISBN 978-1-936402-02-1 hardcover

    Audience: Ages 10 and under.

    1. Imagination & Play — Juvenile fiction. 2. Friendship/Social Issues —
Juvenile fiction. 3. Manners/Social Issues — Juvenile fiction. I. Illust. Hardin, Greg;
Trent, John. II. Title.

Library of Congress Control Number: 2011923167

Printed in the USA
10 9 8 7 6 5 4 3 2 1
First Edition

Free activities for this book are available at www.raventreepress.com

About StinkyKids

From the creative mind of Britt Menzies, a mom who was inspired by her daughter's simple request to paint her as a ballerina, StinkyKids is a brand with a fun, unique, and fresh approach that teaches life lessons through its products and books featuring the 10 diverse StinkyKids characters. The name "StinkyKids" comes from the phrase "little stinkers," which Britt used to describe the innocent behavior of her two kids when they were little.

The StinkyKids characters are little stinkers who learn to make right choices through their childhood mistakes and who live by the motto "Always Be A Leader Of Good." StinkyKids is an innovative brand that appeals to parents for the values it represents and appeals to kids because the characters are real kids getting into real mischief.

Since its inception, StinkyKids donates a percentage of its profits to Books, Bears and Bonnets, Inc., (www.booksbearsbonnets.org), a charity founded in honor of Britt's aunt, who died from uterine cancer. Books, Bears and Bonnets, Inc., delivers gift boxes to children and adults fighting cancer and other life-threatening illnesses.

Come and play with the StinkyKids at www.stinkykids.com!

Love your StinkyKids... they're so stinkin' cute!!

Saturday was Britt's favorite day. It was the day Britt had a playdate with her friends Hannah, Max and Julie. But this Saturday Britt had a secret. A secret she did not want to tell her mommy and daddy. A secret that could stop her favorite playdate from happening.

Hannah and Max were already at Julie's house.
They were pretending to own a haircut shop.
"Let's name our shop 'Haircuts in a Hurry!'"
Julie shouted.
"OK!" replied Max and Hannah.

The doorbell rang. "Britt's here!" Julie said. She ran to
the door. There was Britt, blowing a big bubble with her
gum. She did not look happy.

"We're playing haircut shop, Britt. And you're our first customer!" Hannah said.

Britt plopped into a chair. "Great! Because I have a big problem," Britt said. She blew a big bubble. Max popped it.

Julie used her pretend big girl voice. "And what is your problem, miss? Our famous stylist Hannah can help you!"

Hannah waved her comb in the air. "Is your hair too straight? Do you need a perm?"

"Or too boring? Do you need some color?" Max said.

Britt spit out her gum. "No! My hair is not too straight! My hair is not too boring! My hair is too...

...STICKY!"

"**STICKY?**" yelled Hannah, Julie and Max.
"Yes. **LOOK!**" Britt said. She took down one of
her ponytails. There it was, a huge wad of
gum stuck right in the middle!

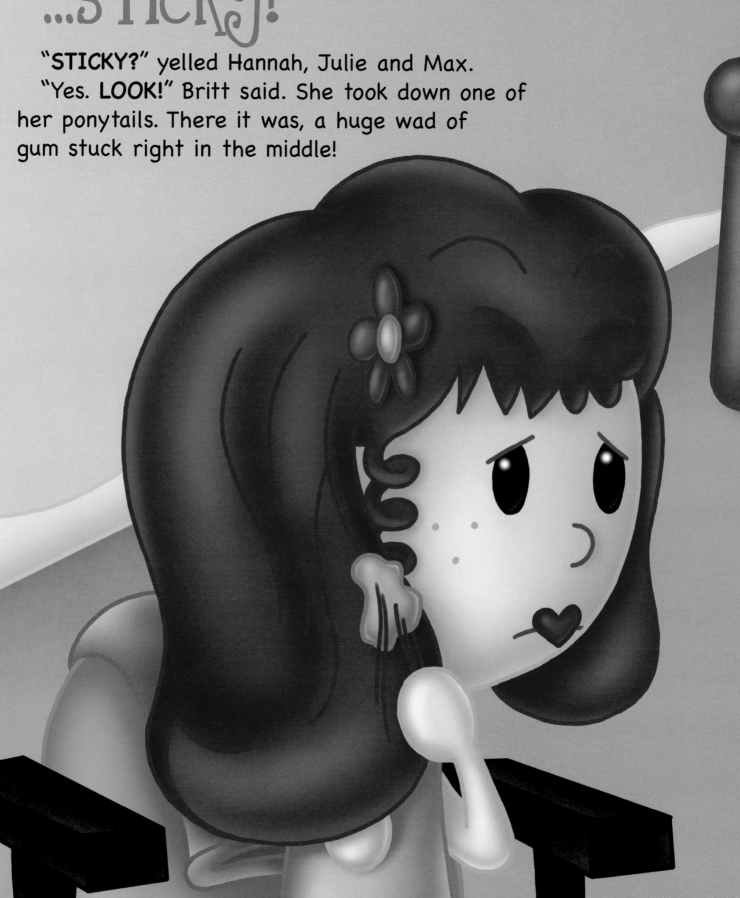

Julie looked shocked. Max got the giggles. But Hannah
said, "I know just what to do. Max... get the peanut butter!"

"Peanut butter will make your hair nice and slippery,
so the gum will just slide out," Hannah said.

Hannah smeared the peanut butter onto the gum in
Britt's hair. She rubbed it all around. Then she licked
her fingers clean, pulled on the gum, and...

...the gum stayed put!

Max looked shocked. Julie got the giggles. But Hannah said, "I know just what to do. Julie... get the ice cubes!"

"Ice cubes will freeze the gum, so it will break into little pieces," Hannah said.

Hannah rubbed ice cubes all around the gum in Britt's hair. She left an ice cube on Britt's head so that the gum would get really cold. She stuck an ice cube in her mouth, pulled on the gum, and...

...the gum stayed put!

Poor Britt felt sick from the smell of peanut butter, and cold from the ice cubes. Her eyes got watery and her nose got sniffly. Her friends tried to make her feel better. Hannah even gave Britt her second favorite puppet to hold. And all four little stinkers tried to think of another plan.

Suddenly Max said, "Hey! I brought my doctor kit!
And in my doctor kit are some..."
"**SCISSORS!**" yelled Hannah, Julie, Britt and Max.

Max got the scissors from his doctor's kit. They were plastic safety scissors. They were not too sharp, but they were just sharp enough to cut hair.

"Great idea!" Britt said. "No more gum in my hair!"

Max cut some of Britt's hair from around the gum. Then he cut some more, and some more, until...

Britt's head looked like a *porcupine!*

Britt covered her face with her hands. "Oh no!" her friends cried. "We're sorry, Britt!"

Britt's shoulders shook and shook. She said, "I... look...

...FUNNY!"

Britt raised her head. She was laughing so hard she could hardly speak.

"Look, Britt's not sad anymore!" Hannah squealed.

"And the gum is out!" shouted Max.

"We did it!" said Julie.

Then the doorbell rang! That stopped their giggles in a hurry! It was Britt's mom, and the playdate was over. The StinkyKids knew they were going to be in trouble!

There was Britt's mom in the doorway. Her eyes were big as she stared at her daughter's porcupine hair. Britt ran to her mom and hugged her.

"I'm sorry, Mommy. I should have told you I had gum in my hair, but I didn't want to miss my playdate. My friends were just trying to help."

Britt's mom stared and stared at Britt's hair. Then she laughed the biggest belly laugh the kids had ever heard. She was remembering a time when she was a little girl with porcupine hair. She laughed so loud that soon all the kids were laughing, too.

Then Britt's mom ran her hand over Britt's hair.
"Well, kids, was this a good choice?" she asked.
The StinkyKids thought for a moment. They thought
about how much fun it was trying to fix Britt's hair.
Then they thought about poor Britt having porcupine
hair for weeks and weeks.
"No, it wasn't," all the StinkyKids said in tiny voices.

"And what should we do about this mess?" Britt's mom asked.
"Um...clean it up?" the StinkyKids said.
The StinkyKids cleaned up the mess they made. There was peanut butter, melted ice, and hair everywhere! It was definitely more fun making the mess than it was cleaning it up.

Britt's mom took her to a real salon to fix her "Haircuts in a Hurry" hairdo. She looked cute as a button when she was done. The lady at the counter let her pick a treat from a huge bowl of candy and gum. Britt was very careful to pick out a lollipop instead of gum.

Britt's dad tucked her into bed that night. They talked about the day's events.

"Britt, sometimes kids need grown-ups to help solve their problems, like getting gum out of hair," he said.

"Okay, Daddy. I'm sorry. I should have told you and Mommy about the gum," Britt said.

"And what's the new rule about scissors?" Britt's dad asked.

"Ask before using!" Britt said. Then she said, "One more kiss, Daddy," in a very tired voice.

He gave her one more kiss and whispered in her ear, "Remember, always be a leader of good."

Just before Britt fell asleep, she remembered she had one more piece of gum left. It was in the drawer of her nightstand, right next to her bed.

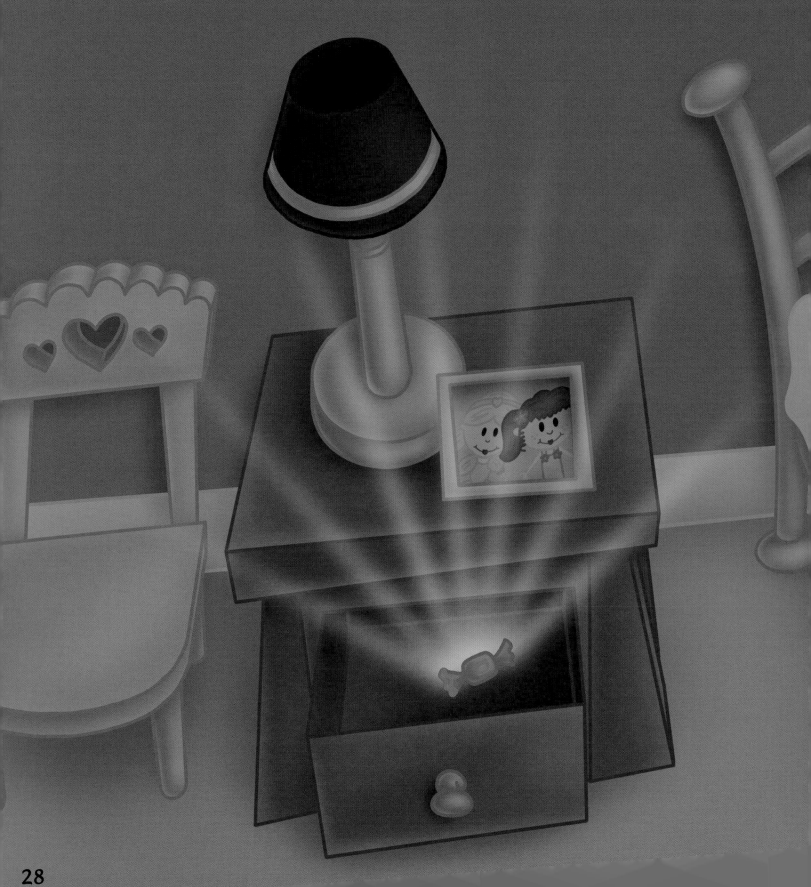

What do *YOU* think happened next?

Dr. Kelli's Parent and Teacher Corner

As an expert on healthy relationships with children who is also a mother and an educator, I am always on the lookout for creative, fun ways to engage children. I was thrilled to meet StinkyKids' creator Britt Menzies and learn about her adorable "Leaders Of Good." StinkyKids stories involve learning through social interaction, creating many opportunities for growth in social development.

StinkyKids® and the Runaway Scissors is a perfect story to engage children in dialogue about making good choices, asking for help when we need it, and taking responsibility for our actions. This story resonates with me personally because I have two little boys that have cut each other's hair — twice. *StinkyKids® and the Runaway Scissors* is refreshing because it shows children that it is okay to make mistakes and demonstrates having the courage to own up to those mistakes. Lastly, it intentionally ends with a question designed to foster ideas from children, sparking interaction between adult and child. We can learn a great deal from our children if we follow their lead and let them express themselves!

Using this Story as a Teaching Tool

It is never too early to start having conversations with children about the things we believe are important. *StinkyKids® and the Runaway Scissors* is a great story to inspire such conversations. An example of a conversation you may have with your children after reading this book is to talk about what you expect them to do if these things ever happen to them. Remember to use statements or open-ended questions to get the most out of your conversations. Here are some topics you and your little stinkers can discuss:

- Oh, no! What could Britt have done to get help?
- I wonder what would happen if you got gum in your hair? What if you were on a play date?
- Scissors in our house/school are not for cutting hair. What do we use scissors for at our house?
- Tell me about a time when you laughed really hard with friends and family.
- What did you notice about the dog?
- How do you look when you are happy? Sad? Proud? Silly? Shocked?
- How would you make a friend feel better?
- What is a secret? When shouldn't you keep a secret?
- What ideas do you have about helping clean up the mess?
- What does it mean to "Always Be A Leader Of Good"?

Suggestions to Further Engage Children

Play is the natural language of children. In addition, children who engage in playtime after a story are more likely to integrate the information and enhance relationships with their parents/teacher/etc. So, in addition to having a discussion about "What do you think happened next?", you may wish to try some focused playtime using toys to let your children express their ideas about the StinkyKids situation.

Takeaway Messages

StinkyKids helps establish and strengthen important messages such as: courage, leadership, making good choices, friendships, self respect, and becoming "Leaders Of Good." Below is a list of takeaway messages from *StinkyKids® and the Runaway Scissors*. Enjoy sharing them with your little stinkers!

- Always ask for help when you need it.
- Parents were kids once and understand childhood mistakes.
- Take responsibility for your actions.
- Clean up your mess.
- Learn from your mistakes.
- Do not go to sleep with gum in your mouth!
- "Always Be A Leader Of Good!"

Dr. Kelli

Kelli B. Ritter, Ph.D.

effective parenting LLC
with Dr. Kelli Ritter

Kelli B. Ritter, Ph.D. is the founder and president of Effective Parenting, LLC in Atlanta, Georgia, and author of *Come Play with Me!*, a guide to using play skills to enhance relationships with children. For more ideas on using play or for information on Dr. Ritter, please visit www.effectiveparentingllc.com.

Introducing...

StinkyKids®
Soft-bodied Dolls

Appropriate for ages 0+

These 12" soft cloth dolls have removable clothing, embroidered faces and personalized tushies.

Each of the ten StinkyKids dolls comes with a bookmark and a trading card explaining their unique personality and talent.

Available at:
madamealexander.com

"Always Be A Leader Of Good"

StinkyKid Skye

Collecting stickers is one of Skye's favorite hobbies. She can draw the best mermaids in her class and always wants ham and cheese sandwiches for lunch. She likes to practice cooking with her friend Joey so she can be a real chef someday.
Leader of Good quality: Keeping in touch with friends and family.

StinkyKid Trey

The golfer of the bunch, Trey is also great at building cool objects out of clay. He likes to take pictures of the places he visits with his big sister Hannah and will sometimes share his French fries with her on their travels.
Leader of Good quality: Caring for the environment.

StinkyKid Hannah

As a future wedding dress designer, Hannah loves to build houses of cards. She creates wonderful puppet shows and serves Granny Smith apples as a snack.
Leader of Good quality: Teaching right from wrong.

StinkyKid Max

A compassionate and caring person, he wants to make people smile by being a professional cartoonist. Max loves to play soccer with his best friend Johnny, and he can do ten chin-ups on his chin-up bar in under one minute. He enjoys a good kosher pickle after his hard work.
Leader of Good quality: Volunteering his services.

StinkyKid Joey

While her doggie Clyde relaxes in the sun, Joey loves to practice hula hooping while wiggling her ears in her backyard. She wants to own an adopt-a-pet shop some day and will serve doggie doughnuts to her furry clients. (Doughnuts are her favorite!)
Leader of Good quality: Compassion towards animals.